SOMETHING IS
GOING TO HAPPEN

SOMETHING IS GOING TO HAPPEN

by Charlotte Zolotow

Pictures by Catherine Stock

Harper & Row, Publishers

Library of Congress Cataloging-in-Publication Data
Zolotow, Charlotte, 1915–
    Something is going to happen.

    Summary: One by one the members of a family awake
one cold November morning to discover that during the
night there has been a beautiful snowfall.
    [1. Snow—Fiction]   I. Stock, Catherine, ill.
II. Title.
PZ7.Z77Sq   1988   [E]   87-26661
ISBN 0-06-027028-4
ISBN 0-06-027029-2 (lib. bdg.)

SOMETHING IS
GOING TO HAPPEN

"Something is going to happen this morning," the mother thought when she woke up.

She lay in bed a moment more, listening to the bare branch of the maple tree tapping against the bedroom window.

Everyone was sleeping.

Outside, the cold November wind blew with a low whining sound.

The father was still asleep.

The little boy was still asleep.

The little girl was still asleep.

Even the little black dog was still sleeping.

"It's just an ordinary Monday," the mother thought,
"but I know something is going to happen. I feel it."
And she began dressing quietly, leaving the shades
pulled down so as not to wake the father yet.

Then she tiptoed down to the kitchen. It was still dark outside, and she turned on the light.

The father opened his eyes.

He lay in bed listening to the wind and to the maple branch tapping the windowpane.

"Something is going to happen this morning," he thought.

He got out of bed.

The little girl was still asleep.

The little boy was still asleep.

Even the little dog was still sleeping.

"Something is going to happen," the father thought.

"I feel it."

The father could hear the mother downstairs in the kitchen as he turned on the light and began to get dressed. The smell of fresh coffee and warm vanilla from muffins baking filled the house.

"Something is going to happen this morning," the little boy thought when he woke up. He lay in bed thinking of the day before. It had been so bleak. The last of the autumn leaves had long since turned brown, the last of the big crinkling leaves had been raked into piles. The few leaves left blew dismally across the frozen earth in the cold wind. Nothing had happened for so long! He shivered and got out of bed.

The little boy turned on the light. He could hear his
mother and father having coffee in the kitchen.

His school clothes were folded on the chair, and he began to dress. He pulled his heavy sweater over his head and smelled the freshly baked muffins, and he hurried to comb his hair.

"Something is going to happen," he thought again. "I feel it."

Now the little girl opened her eyes.

She heard the wind whining around the house as she got out of bed.

"Something is going to happen this morning," she thought, rubbing her eyes.

The house was filled with the smell of coffee and
warm muffins, and she could hear dishes rattling in the
kitchen.

A thin sliver of light from the hall lamp showed
under her door.

She was too little to go to school.

She was too little to dress herself.

So she put on her fuzzy bedroom slippers.

She put on her warm woolen bathrobe.

"Something is going to happen," she thought again,
listening to the whining of the wind. "I feel it."

Downstairs she could hear her father snap his briefcase closed before he left for the office.

She could hear her brother whistling to himself as he got his books together for school.

She could hear her mother rattling hangers in the
closet, finding coats and gloves and mufflers before
they went out into the whining November wind.

And she could hear the little dog waking up.

First he snorted and shook his head.

Then he yawned.

Then he stretched himself: front paws, back paws.

Then he climbed down from the foot of the bed.

Then he stood still.

There was something strange.

His ears stood up straight as he listened.

The wind had suddenly stopped.

There was only the sound of the little girl going downstairs one step at a time to say good-bye to her father going to work and good-bye to her brother going to school.

The little dog sniffed the air again, standing quite
still. All he smelled in the house was people smell and
muffin smell and coffee smell.

He pattered down the stairs quickly and reached the front door just as the father opened it to go out.

"Look what happened!" the father said.

"Look!" said the little boy.

"Look!" said the little girl.

"Look!" said the mother.

The little dog pushed his way through their legs and looked.

Slowly drifting through the air were thousands of white icy flakes. They had settled on the ground and covered the world with white. The earth was white, the bushes were white, the trees were white, the sidewalk was white, the road was white, the porch stairs were white, and as the little black dog ran down the path into the falling snow, he began to turn white too.